Me and My Mates

Aidan Macfarlane and A[...] in Oxford. They have al[...] bestsellers – *The Diary of a Teenage [Health] [Freak]* [and] *I'm a Health Freak Too!*, as well as *Mum – I Feel Funny!*, which won the Times Educational Supplement information book award.

They have carried out extensive academic research into teenagers and their attitudes and health problems. Much of the information in their writing is based on this research.

Aidan Macfarlane is divorced and has three teenage children. He is a consultant paediatrician with a special interest in teenage health. He has published widely in the medical field, including *The Psychology of Childbirth* and *A Pocket Consultant of Child Health*.

Ann McPherson is married with three children – two teenagers and one who has just completed the course. She is a general practitioner who looks after many teenagers. She is author of *Women's Problems in General Practice* and, with Ann Oakley and Helen Roberts, of *Miscarriage*.

Sarah Garland is a writer and illustrator of children's books, shortlisted for the Best Baby Book of 1990, and currently working on a graphic thriller. She has four children. Three of them are teenagers who have provided vital research material for this book.

Also by Aidan Macfarlane and
Ann McPherson

The Diary of a Teenage Health Freak
I'm a Health Freak Too!
Mum – I Feel Funny!

Aidan Macfarlane
and
Ann McPherson

Me and My Mates

Illustrations by Sarah Garland

Pan Original
London, Sydney and Auckland

First published in 1991 by Pan Books Ltd,
Cavaye Place, London SW10 9PG

9 8 7 6 5 4 3 2 1

ISBN 0 330 31615 X

Phototypeset by Input Typesetting Ltd., London
Printed and bound in Great Britain by
Clays Ltd, St Ives plc, Bungay, Suffolk

Contents

Acknowledgements

The sources of this book were numerous – friends, their children, journals, books, the readers of *Just Seventeen*, our children, their friends, medical colleagues, members of an Oxford church youth group, and the Sticky Fingers. We would like to acknowledge some people individually but given the somewhat sensitive nature of some of the subject material dealt with in the book we felt their identities should be protected. Any similarity between the characters in the book and any living person is purely and absolutely coincidental – so you can stop trying to guess. After all, although we are all meant to be individuals – we also do have a lot in common!

There are some we can name. Marny Leech for remaining an essential ingredient – with her sureness in making all the details consistent, her patience with our spelling and 'English' and sure knowledge of what the readers will and will not accept; Marion Lloyd for finally giving in to what we wanted with such good grace; and Sarah Garland for enriching our text with humorous and perceptive drawings of our teenage characters – we feel that we can at last 'see' them. Klim, who has not only tolerated teenage behaviour itself but now has to tolerate it second hand via the books. Sam, Magnus, Tess, Tamara, Beth and Gus who, although not exactly revealing aspects of their own lives, made sure that our observations fell in line with their views of teenage existence.

Aidan Macfarlane and Ann McPherson

1 Steve's turn-on

'Listen patsy face, if I really want the whole world to know something then all I have to do is tell you it's a secret. You're a motor-mouth when you get going, or was it just the beer talking this time? Half a pint and half the world knows everything – a pint and the other half suddenly discovers it.'

'Don't be so bloody naïve – wasn't much of a secret anyway. You're like the government. Anything

you know has to be classified under the Official
Secrets Act, whereas even the local cats know Tony
got off with Rachel last night. The reason you're
trying to keep it quiet is that you'd like to get off
with her yourself.'

Nothing will ever stop my sister Di's mouth, so life
certainly wasn't in great shape for me given the
amount that I didn't want discussed at this moment.
What I wanted was for everyone to shut up and talk
about something else, but then my mum – who's
always into all our business – turned to me saying,
'You're not much of a one to talk, from what I've
been hearing about you.'

As I say, the last thing I wanted anyone to talk
about was me and the previous night. It was a full-
time occupation – taking completely blinding concentration – not to think about it myself.

I hate parties. I worry non-stop about what they're
going to be like for hours ahead – and I was partly
responsible for this one. How I got into it all I don't
know. I'd asked Mum to drive me down to the local
Cash and Carry. The idea – from the teachers – was
that I should buy some of the drink. They thought a
big bottle of beer or two would be about right, but
I hadn't told Mum that. Tony, Will and Dan had got
me at break and said that beer was for wimps and
what about half a dozen bottles of vodka to go into
a punch? It didn't sound totally safe but I tried to be
casual with Mum when she asked what I needed. It

came out as 'Four bottles of something or other', not revealing exactly what. Luckily she sent me off to get them, so in went six bottles of vodka, sort of accidentally covered up with twenty-five packets of crisps, nuts and things. At the check-out I asked Mum to go and get some paper plates, to stop her seeing the bottles being rocked along the conveyor. When the total came up, Mum started to say something about how the price of beer must have gone up but then she thought better of it. Just groaned and flashed her 'Cash and Carry' card. Oh, for my own bit of plastic.

Mum offered to hump the load down to the school with me. Dilemma. Didn't fancy a three-mile ride with all that stuff on my back, upsetting my centre of gravity and offering a distinct danger to life, limb and ace racing bike alike. On the other hand, I wanted to be free to come home when *I* wanted – rather than have Mum collect me at a 'reasonable hour' like 10.30 p.m. Compromise. Got Mum to take everything except the vodka – which I discreetly stuffed into my cycle bags. I had a quick shave – too quick, as I nicked the edge of my lip and blood flowed everywhere. I tried to disguise it with a piece of lav paper, but it was like holding back the bursting Dutch dykes. I was totally disfigured. Maybe I wouldn't go to the party after all – but I had to because of the drink.

I 'borrowed' Dad's best suit jacket to go with my 501s. There had been a vote for 'smart dress' – whatever that means. Bike lights were a problem. Usually the rear one fits in my back trouser pocket, but my 501s seemed to have shrunk. After a few breathing exercises I managed to expand them enough to make room. The front light I stuck on to the handlebars with Sellotape. Loud moans from Mum and Dad about it being against the law. Rode off ignoring them. Could do the journey with my eyes closed – including just missing Mr Brock in the playground – it's the same every day.

I parked my bike behind one of the ten portakabins that make up half the school buildings. It doesn't seem to me that much of my parents' tax money gets directed towards *my* education. It goes into obsolete, redundant nukes instead.

Our 'hall' looked as if it had been designed as a warehouse for second-hand furniture, and it hadn't seen a coat of paint for twenty years. I think it's held together by the GCSE and 'A' level 'works of art' pinned all over the walls. Jerry's GCSE self-portrait makes her look almost human – it was done before her mohican hairstyle but when she was already wearing her plastic 'skull' ear-rings.

I smashed one of the bottles as I was taking my panniers off – probably not half a bad thing seeing what a disaster the punch turned out to be.

The entire fifth year was completely plastered. A wall to wall wipe-out. They're a pretty obnoxious lot at the best of times but when tanked up – uncontroll-able. The teachers were out in force trying to round them up like Texas rangers. No doubt the head will act like a sheriff when she hears about it. Would probably like to flog the lot of them and hang them from the window of the sixth-form common room. There was food flying everywhere – chicken legs, bags of crisps, half buns. Dennis Brock, who used to teach me maths last year, went over the top – lost his cool completely, sweaty faced, shouting. He man-handled a couple of the worst offenders – I'm sur-prised they didn't lose their manhoods (personally, I think the boys could sue for GBH). There was vomit

and pee in the lavatories, mixed with a faint whiff of dope. My mates are mad to mess with that stuff. Every male teacher taking a leak must have known what was going on.

All the sixth-form committee were meant to have been there early to help arrange things. Faithful old Rachel, the ever-devoted (or should it be devout?) David and me got there at six. Always the same

martyred group who actually do the things they say
they will. Meanwhile the likes of Tony and Will, who
were so full of how we must do this and that at
break, failed to show again. Maybe it's because we
like being martyrs. Maybe too it's the same for the
teachers. Mr Brock, Mr Coots and Miss Smaker
always get landed with these parties, whereas the
head, Mrs Boon, promises but never quite makes it.

Could be I will go through the whole of life being like this. I sometimes wish I was the one who didn't turn up, but I don't think I have the guts.

Funny really. David, Tony and myself were inseparable at our first school – we were even known as 'the terrible triplets', all blond-haired and in the same

form. It wasn't till we got to upper school that our true characters started to emerge. Tony began to get all the street cred – everyone wanted to be around him and those who weren't, like me, felt they were missing out on something. HE was where it was all happening. I think his image began to fall apart in the fifth year. He made us all feel like groffs because we did at least try and do some work – while he was out in town showing up at all the gatherings. Then came the GCSE results. Although he did manage to get a few GCSEs, they were too many to have real street cred and too few to be admired by the rest of us. In fact, he blew it.

Looking at David helping prepare for the party, staggering around under a swaying pile of metal and canvas chairs, I thought he hadn't changed much – except he was being lashed by his hormones and had grown bigger. In fact he was a heavy-weight elephant. He was dressed up for the occasion, whiter than white shirt and even cuff-links. Very smart image – but definitely not for me. We're still good friends, though I don't understand a thing about him.

I was lost in these musings when David fell over with a crash and a cry of 'sh ... it'. It seemed a fairly efficient, if noisy, way of distributing a hundred chairs – even if Mr Brock thought that smaller stacks might help. We sweated away – put more and more chairs out, then tables; then David and Rachel put tablecloths on and a few plates. Sue and Paul had arrived and were putting up decorations. Glasses began to appear, paper napkins, streamers, bottles with candles in them. God, I thought, we'll never make it. Suddenly someone lit a few candles and turned the lights off. I couldn't believe it. What an hour before had been a bare, cold, clangy, smelly concentration camp, doubling as a school hall where we all had to take roll-call in the mornings, had suddenly turned into a warm, wonderful, intimate, candle-lit café just made for smooching.

That was all fine – but it was 7.40, the party was meant to have started ten minutes ago, and there wasn't a person in sight. Hey, this was *my* party – or rather it was being organized by the lower sixth for the fifth and sixth forms, but I felt responsible. Last year's had been the greatest to date, even if all future parties were nearly banned. And here we were with this one on our plate – help!

What was worse was having to talk to the teachers. Pure embarrassment – didn't know what to say. They weren't much help either.

Hullo Steven –
how's your sister Di?

She's fine thank you,
Miss Smaker.

Good – what's she doing
at the moment?

She's working at the
local Co-op on the desk.

That's good –
is she enjoying it?

Yes, Miss Smaker,
but it's not for always.

This could have gone on for ever, and my stomach

was turning to lead. I could see other little talking groups – looking like squeaking penguins. Suddenly Tony appeared, weighed down under clinking cases, his long scraggly hair gone orange with henna. His black leather jacket had more veins in it than Mrs Boon's legs. (I should know – we've all had to study them at every Monday assembly for the last five years.) His 'designer' jeans were so torn that there was more of Tony's flesh to be seen than material – and unwashed flesh at that. At least he was wearing a black bow-tie.

He signalled for me to go over. Even after all these years, off I trotted. I felt honoured at the attention – I'm such a creep. All he wanted was the six (now five) bottles of vodka, and me to help him with the punch. I could hardly bear to watch what was going in. Tony must be a sucker to film advertising. There was a bottle of everything that any beautiful woman has ever drunk on any screen advert ever made. I can't understand why at school we have whole 'social guidance' classes devoted to the evils of alcohol, while in the cinema – even at PGs – we're subjected to an endless barrage of sexy ladies telling us how hard we'd be if we drank Bacardi rum, Pernod, Cinzano, and every other concoction found on those so-called 'desert islands' (containing them and a camera crew of sixteen plus a supporting cast of thousands). Maybe the hypocrisy of the government will allow adverts showing beautiful broads shooting themselves up with heroin in the future?

By the time we'd finished with the punch I was surprised it didn't go in for spontaneous combustion and explode. I have to admit I was dead worried, but Tony handed round the glasses like a professional bar-tender saying, 'Nothing very strong', 'Just to get the party going', 'Make you feel a bit happy' – whereas I was thinking, 'We'll have to pick you up off the floor', 'It'll pickle you for ever and even the maggots will get drunk', 'Your mother will never recognize you

again' and, worst of all, 'They'll all blame me'.

While all this was going on, a gradual buzz started to impinge on my slavering conscience. Things were stirring in the outer reaches of the assembly-hall-cum-café. The beginnings of nuclear fission – or just the effects of the punch? I wasn't ready to face this yet. I felt exhausted after our heroic efforts to get it all together and my relief that things were beginning to happen at last. I squinted into my plastic mug of evil brew. Perhaps a sip wouldn't hurt? It didn't. Tony was a real sorcerer. The taste was a mixture of sweet plastic disgustingnesses – a sort of liquid candyfloss that flowed through my blood and blew the top off my head. Suddenly the world looked infinitely less bleak. Tony went off to smoke in the lavatories leaving a 'free for all' around the drinks. He wanted me to join him for a joint of ganja – as he's told me he hates smoking alone. I didn't go. I know I still jump when Tony commands – but there has to be some point where I stop.

Normally Mr Smythe, head of chemistry, who probably hasn't missed an upper school party in the last hundred years, would have been responsible for the C_2H_5OH distribution, but he's away sick and none of the other teachers seemed to want to take it on. Didn't realize one needed a degree in chemistry to mix drinks – Tony seemed to do all right with a GCSE 'N'!

I noticed Rachel looking at Tony as he disappeared. Surely she can't fancy HIM? I fancy her, whatever she wears. For instance, I'd normally think that high heels were cheap – but on her, well, she looked a princess. The hairdo too – not just your second-hand 'Lady Di' creation – just original Rachel, and terrific at that. She thinks of me as a 'good friend', always around when a shoulder is needed to cry on, or when she wants some company to do something with. I've always wanted it to go a bit further, but there just never seems to be the opening

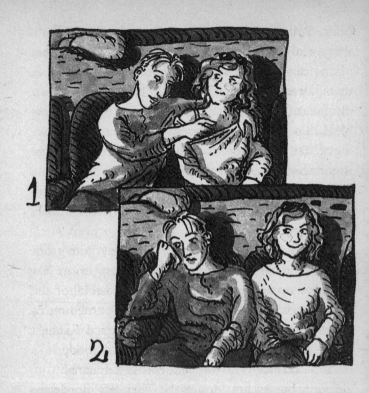

Anything faintly suggestive on my part (like trying to fumble her breasts in the back of the cinema) she treats as a joke. She doesn't seem to see that I really want her. She doesn't seem to see me at all. Not that I've broken any frankness records in trying to tell her about my feelings.

I felt a right wallflower stuck watching everyone else having such a fantastic time. David's new image was a winner with the girls. At one time or another he seemed to be dancing with every decent-looking sixth-former available. What's he got that I haven't? Maybe my nicked lip was the problem. I kept picking the piece of lav paper off and must have looked worse than Dracula dripping blood. The night wore on. Bright embarrassed laughter turned to intimate conversation and was well on its way to body contact. But I was getting nowhere. I couldn't break into that solid mass of female talk and titivation.

Then at last the scene changed. One moment I was near suicide, the next I was locked in a sexy dance with Jerry. Hearing her on the sax had been a real turn-on. I finished up dancing with her quite a few times – though there was a lot of competition. She snuggled up against me so that I could feel all of her. Every nerve cell in my skin was being turned on by every point of contact. I'd have preferred Rachel's body though – Jerry's like that with everybody.

At 11 o'clock everyone suddenly disappeared. Cinderellas, but an hour too early. They left more mess though than the odd shoe, a few rats and a pumpkin. It looked just like the local council tip on a Saturday. And who was left to clear the dump up? A 'dear and faithful' band of pissed idiots – David, me, Sue and Paul, and (total surprise) 'had by everybody' Jerry, who by this time was into David.

It had been a long evening and I was disastrously tired. I wanted to give up thinking about it all – but couldn't. The fact that Tony had disappeared was no surprise, but I didn't like the fact that Rachel was absent too. Two thoughts like this occurring together can set smut-like excrescences of suspicion crawling between my mind modules, not helped by Rachel being so unfriendly when I danced with her. I seem to be about as attractive to her as boiling water is to a lobster.

The teachers slopped around totally irritated. They thought half the problem was the people who'd arrived at the party already half tanked-up. I'm glad they hadn't realized that the main problem was that evil, vodka-laden, witches' brew. (They must have livers like hard-boiled eggs not to have felt the effects themselves. Maybe you have to be a near-alcoholic to want to be a teacher nowadays?) Nothing will stop me from feeling guilty, but it was unfair them being so bloody-minded to us, when we were the ones helping! I suppose their dislike of the evening's happenings had to be off-loaded on to someone, and that 'someone' was us.

They did at least offer some bad-tempered help. The caretaker had taken one look at the lavatories and said there was no way HE was going anywhere near THEM. So it was poor shitty little me who was sent off to recce the damage. Apart from the toilet rolls stuck down them, there were dirty paper plates, fag ends, broken bottles, sodden pieces of clothing lying around; and a few semi-conscious mounds of what might, tomorrow, just pass for humanity. It didn't seem too bad at first – just average partyish –

until I saw and smelt the sick. It made me gag and
gag again – foul, foul, foul. I really hate people –
even my friends.

2 Rachel nearly goes too far

Steve's nice enough. It's good for my ego to have someone so devoted. I know he wants to be serious, but it's not what I want. How can I tell him I just want to be friends and that it doesn't always have to be sex? Even kissing and stuff – I just don't fancy it with him.

ACE party – started getting ready for it as soon as I got up. The real fun of parties for me is thinking about it all in advance – what I'm going to wear, my make-up, who's going to get off with who – all stuff like that. It always seems to be me who helps get the place itself ready. Maybe because I don't actually like the parties themselves half so much. This one was different though.

As usual, Mum and Dad wanted to know all about it. Who was I going with? Was there going to be alcohol? What time would I be back? Was Miranda going to be there? Mum insisted that it wasn't that she wanted to stop me doing anything – she was just interested. Maybe it's because she's a teacher and thinks she knows everything we get up to, but she's only primary, and the way she treats me it shows. At least Dad's a bit more worldly – maybe because he travels a lot with his charity work and sees how people in other countries treat their children.

Once the party got going, I stayed away from the usual group – Steve, David, Paul, Sue and co. First time I've talked to Tony, Will and Dan for years. Tony, David and Steve used to be really close. Tony's such a people user. Everyone hero-worships him which he loves, and then when he hasn't any need for them any more he just drops them. It's fun being with him though. There's something dangerous about him. He's always nearly getting into trouble, always taking risks, totally against authority. There's something about him I almost admire, and yet I totally disapprove of his selfishness. He just does his own thing, whoever gets hurt – and it's never him.

Steve was his usual self – sniffing around me as if I was a bitch on heat. When I ignored him, he looked pathetic and hurt. He spent the whole time picking at the corner of his mouth and then rushing off to the lav. He's really getting on my nerves. Even the way he was dressed annoyed me, though normally he dresses quite well. Why can't he let go – like Tony – wear leathers or something and be a bit less conventional.

I had a chat with Jerry. I wish I dared look so outrageous, mohican hair and all. She's fed up with Tony, thinks he just uses her, like all men do. She suddenly told me something awful that her uncle did when she was little. Usually I'm quite a tolerant person, but I think men like that should be castrated. Jerry said that if you were to do that, there wouldn't be anyone left to carry on the human race. She's pretty cynical.

I'd suddenly had enough of always helping. For once, Steve and co were going to have to do without me. It was Tony who was making me feel good. He seemed so much more mature than the other boys around. Someone I could get excited over. He said he was bored with the party, felt he'd done his bit and wanted to cut out. He casually asked if I wanted to come too, and if so to meet him outside in ten minutes. I couldn't believe he meant it – but then he and Jerry seemed to be breaking up, and I certainly

owed Steve nothing. I heard myself saying 'Yes', but maybe I was a bit pissed because I slipped over in a pool of something on the floor and tore Mum's dress. I also let Tony drive me to a house where there was another party going on. I must have been mad driving with him as he'd been drinking, like everyone else. Mum would kill me if she knew. (It's lucky *he* didn't kill me first.)

I can't remember much of what happened next – or maybe I'd prefer to forget. It was a huge bleak house, with glaring lights and blaring people in some rooms, and darkness and murmuring, heaving bodies in others. Tony and I joined a crowd jammed into a long kitchen. Everyone was trying to get to the sink, which was full of wine and broken plastic cups. The floor was all sticky where wine had got spilt, and it glued me to it every time I took a step.

Tony knew everyone – making me feel completely out of it. Finally he took me off to dance in total blackness. He kept pressing himself up against me and feeling me up, putting his hands everywhere.

Suddenly I didn't want to be there any more. I wanted to get away. I felt sick. I knew Tony had a terrible reputation for trying to sleep with anyone he laid hands on – and he was certainly doing that to me. I suppose my reputation will be nil now anyhow – but this wasn't something I wanted to get into.

Some people treat sex in a far more casual way than others. Personally, I treat sex as something special, not to be taken for granted. Maybe I'm old-fashioned, but I feel it's wrong to 'jump into bed' with everyone you go out with. It makes me sick when I see and hear about the casual sex going on today. It is worrying where the future is concerned too, because when I do decide to settle down and have a sexual relationship with someone, the worry of the person having AIDS will always be with me.

Sleeping with someone really means something to me. I think you have to be involved with someone to go to bed with them. This is important to me – quite apart from the risks involved. But given that there's no cure for AIDS, and Tony's a dead bad sort, the risks were there. I'm sure he sleeps around, and I bet he never asks girls who they've slept with. Maybe he's even into men, and I'm sure he's experimented with drugs. You never know with someone like Tony. He wants to try everything.

It was awful – one moment I was enjoying myself, and the next I felt as if I was dancing with a leper. I pushed Tony away and walked out, saying I needed some fresh air – which I did! What a shit. When I went back in he'd disappeared, absolutely vanished. Why did I think he'd be any different with me? I was just another in a long line of people he couldn't care less about as soon as he realized they wouldn't do what he wanted.

The worst thing was that I had to walk home. What a sight, tottering along on Miranda's high heels which I had to take off, Mum's dress torn up the side, my mascara all run because I'd started crying. I had to throw up in someone's front garden. Not very pleasant for them when they came out to admire their geraniums in the morning. I think I hit their gnome by mistake. To my relief no one raped me (not even the gnome). When I got back, I sat on my bed for I don't know how long trying to repair Mum's dress, getting the mud and so on off the high heels, and having a good cry.

Waking up this morning was the worst thing that could have happened to me. Yes, the party had been 'great'. But what an end to the evening. Please God, can I have the end again and change it?

I was glad I'd not done what Tony wanted though. When I do decide to lose my virginity, I'll choose carefully, and I'll want the bloke to make a long-term commitment to me, and I'll only sleep with him when he has. I might even insist that he has an AIDS test first, just to make sure. I know it's very sad not being able to trust someone you love, but my life's too important to waste when a simple test could save it. Even if there was a cure for AIDS, I would still play it safe because of all the other things you can catch. I'm certainly not going to lose my virginity to some Tony character at a strange party when I'm drunk. Funny, but doing some things makes you feel as if you've lost your virginity even if you haven't. It gives you a sort of dirty feeling.

Mum must be psychic or something. Started asking me at breakfast, as my rice crispies were blasting my headache to pieces with their 'snap, crackle and pop', whether there was anyone at school I thought was particularly at risk of catching AIDS – either from sleeping around or from injecting drugs. Everybody seems to be thinking of only one thing (me included). AIDS, AIDS, AIDS – even at breakfast. I can't actually get it into my brain that it will happen to anyone I know, but then you never think *you're* going to be in a plane crash.

Don't know why, but I suddenly burst out laughing because I realized, looking at Mum, that Grandma and Grandpa must have done it sometime to produce her. I mean, there's no way they could do it now – what with Grandpa's hip and all that. Though I suppose it's not his hip but some other more floppy bit of him that he'd be worrying about. There should be a law against anyone doing it over the age of fifty.

What does worry me a bit at the moment is what Dad might be up to, with him being away working abroad so much. There was this serial on telly about a man who'd caught AIDS from a prostitute in Africa while on a business trip. Week after week we saw him getting worse and worse. Then we saw him having to tell his family, and they all found out at work. He got the push and the whole family got dragged down by it. It seems that the disease is so common in men and women in parts of Africa that in some places half of all the pregnant women carry the virus. Maybe seeing how awful it is will persuade people here to use the proper precautions to stop it spreading so fast. I couldn't bear it if something like that happened in our family.

3 Tony exposed to hard drugs

Dad used to make me a really fabulous fry-up every morning before he pushed off. Nowadays Mum just about manages coffee and toast before disappearing off to work. Leaves me to get myself together for school. Once she'd left the kitchen, I had a quick fag and coughed all the way to the bus-stop. Too late as usual and missed the bus. If I went to bed earlier I might occasionally get to school on time. Pity I flogged my bike – but was so short of the readies it was the only way to survive. I conned some fourth-former who knew nothing about bikes so paid me twice as much as it was worth. Luckily the world is full of fools – including Steve, who bought Bob's bike. It was an ace racer, which I wouldn't have minded myself if I didn't suspect that it might have fallen off the back of a lorry. Mum's given up trying to keep me in pocket-money or in bikes (they either get flogged or nicked). Just gives me an allowance at the beginning of each month, which I've already spent by the end of the previous month – because I'm always so much in debt to all my friends.

By a smooth chance Mr Brock suddenly appeared in his car – late too, so I thumbed a lift. He definitely wanted to pretend he hadn't seen me but I stepped in front of his car at the red light so he had to give me a lift or run me over. I know which he would've preferred to have done. He wouldn't say a blind thing to me except how much he wasn't looking forward to the party this evening. Said nothing myself.

School's given up caring what time I turn up now I'm in the lower sixth. In fact I wish they'd mind a bit more. Just someone to take some notice would be nice.

Dan, Will and I got Steve in a corner during break. He always does what he's told ever since we were in primary together. Probably because I beat the shit out of him the first term – and he knows I'd do it again should the need occur. I put in an order for six

bottles of vodka as his mum has a 'Cash and Carry' card. Threatened to tell his mum about the time he had a puff of one of my joints last year. Case of the 'word' being mightier than a smash on the nose. Jerry thinks I'm a right bastard getting Steve to do my dirty work. I'll have to show her I don't like her attitude – she used to back me up completely. I'm all for women's lib but they have to be shown. As for Steve, he's always giving me a whole lot of crap about relationships with women – as if he'd know anything. I don't think you can learn about girls unless you really experience them. Some kids think you can pick it all up by reading magazines and books – but I don't think you learn a thing from them. It's the day-to-day business of actually getting on with someone and knowing what they like and don't like that counts.

Skived off in the afternoon as I hadn't done the work for Mrs Pole who'd set me a whole lot of stuff for my resit of geography. Heavy night last night with Jerry. Think she's two-timing me with a friend of Miranda's. Miranda and her being thick as thieves is bad news. Means I can't get away with anything. Fell asleep as soon as I got home. Woke at 7.30 p.m. and called Jerry but she'd gone. I'd missed helping get the place at school ready – but they knew I'd never make it. The wimps will be there slaving away, making themselves feel indispensable.

Was about to crash down to the pub when I remembered I'd promised to do the punch, so only had a quick pint at home. Wonder why Mr Smythe is off sick? He usually does the drinks at these do's. Last time he was in he asked me to help out. Only teacher who seems to have any trust in me. Funny bloke, always a loner but he's away sick a lot these days. No one knows what's the matter with him. Staff won't say – why the secrecy? Maybe we're driving him to have a nervous breakdown.

Bleak scene when I got to school – meant to be a party but felt like my grandad's funeral. There was no way a few balloons and the odd paper tablecloth were going to disguise that Nissen hut. They should've saved the money and spent it on more drink. Being blind drunk was the only way to improve this lot. I set to work and made the punch I've nicknamed 'Tony's Pan Galactic Gargleblaster' in honour of *Hitch-hiker's Guide*. The *Encyclopaedia Galactica* is right. My drink is just like 'having your brains smashed out by a slice of lemon wrapped round a large gold brick', except mine is much better because you don't feel the subtle smash of the brick until about half an hour after you've drunk it.

Had a couple of glasses as a taster – fab stuff, I can take any amount of it. Ate some of what someone referred to as 'food' and left for a smoke in the lav. After all, I'd done enough to justify my free ticket. Eyed a few of the girls but I prefer them more mature, like Miranda. Not that I ever got anywhere when I went out with her but I'm still sorry she's left.

Jerry was a real pain in the arse all evening. Refused to dance with me, just sulked or played bimbo by flirting with Paul and Steve. As if I cared. Decided 'perfect' Rachel was to be the woman of the evening for me. She may not have Jerry's looks, but she's certainly got more brains. It's time she found out what life is about, and who better to show her than me? Insider knowledge that Adrian was having a decent gathering at his parents' house while they're away, so got Rachel tanked up on a couple of glasses of Gargleblaster before we left, and had another one myself. Women are always easier to land when they're plastered. Also, nothing like having Mum's car to impress them. Just as well she's in London with her boyfriend for the evening. Can't have her knowing I've borrowed it again. She wasn't too impressed by the two tyres I carved up on the kerb last week on the way back from the pub. Cost her a packet. She wanted me to pay, but knew that was no deal.

At Adrian's – Rachel wouldn't play. I tried everything. I was getting really worked up but it turned out she was just another bloody cockteaser. Suddenly wouldn't even kiss me properly. Maybe she thought she'd catch something. So much for that. I wasn't going to stick around and wait for that cold fish so decided she'd just have to walk home. It was turning into a real dick of a night and I needed something to give me a lift.

Met Jack on my way out who was going on somewhere. He said I could come too if I'd give him a ride. We drove miles into the back of beyond. Nowhere I'd been before and I certainly wouldn't want to find it again, as Jack's scene turned out to be heavier than even I'd reckoned with. It was above a garage – not much noise going on except coughing and groaning and a low mutter. Took me some time to make anything out. Man, those guys must be mad. I'd thought of Jack as a cool dude till tonight. But when he began shooting up with the rest of them, I knew this scene wasn't for me.

I'd barely got a foot inside the door when some bloke tried to score me off with some crack. Did I want that hook for life? No thanks. I'll try most things but . . . Worst was a woman asking around to borrow someone else's works. Didn't think even this crowd of mainliners would share syringes, needles or any of the rest of the stuff that goes with drug-taking. Supposing she's pregnant and gives something to her kid? Just unbelievable what some people will do. Maybe they think none of them are HIV positive, but how would they know? Shooting up, sharing needles, smoking crack – this was all way beyond me and I cut out of there at speed. I was trembling and cold when I got outside – takes a lot to make me feel a total innocent. I'd seen too much on telly about how it's now the commonest way of getting AIDS – injecting yourself with drugs using other people's needles.

If I got AIDS, I think I'd feel pretty angry about it, and that if I was going to die I might just as well go out and spread it to other people. The way I feel about Jerry at the moment, she'd be the first.

Anyhow, I don't think it'll ever happen to me. I'm the lucky sort and always get away with it. After all, the last time the police raided a pub I was in everyone got picked up but me. I managed to slip out and not get done. You have to take chances in life. That's what life is all about. People take it too seriously. It takes all the fun away. I'm into having fun with anyone else who's game. Anyway, I think contraception is the girl's responsibility – condoms just spoil it. They're old-fashioned. And they don't always work – how do you think I was conceived?

Personally I get totally confused sometimes. I can read three articles in any one day in the newspaper, each giving contradictory opinions. I mean, how are you to know what the risks really are when you've got one lot of people saying you've got to use condoms all the time, another group saying not to have sex at all (just wank instead I suppose), and a third group saying it's OK to do whatever you want.

Anyhow, I wouldn't turn to my mother for advice. I'm not comfortable around her talking about that stuff, plus I know my mum isn't comfortable with that chat either. I wouldn't get any straight answers.

About condoms, well I suppose so. Most of the time girls want me to use a condom, but I don't use one if I can help it. I just don't think too much about getting a dose.

I thought about all this as I was driving home. I suddenly realized that I'd got back OK, but had no idea what way I'd driven or anything – totally out of it.

4 David reflects the risks

I certainly didn't get up with any halo round my head
this morning, though I'm sometimes depressed by the
way the rest of the world thinks I do (or should)
every morning. I probably don't go to church much
more than other people. But I do have the burden of
feeling extra guilty. Someone like Tony doesn't care
whether he does what he says he will or not – while
I *have* to do something if I say I'm going to – not

just because I believe in God but also because of the way my parents are. When we all agreed to help getting things organized for the party – even though I'd arranged to have a kick around with the rest of the football team – it was the 'duty' which came first. Steve was there and so was Rachel, Paul and Sue, but I wish Jerry had come early too. If she could just get away from Tony's influence a bit, I'm sure she'd be happier and I could help her.

We all mucked about a bit – me tossing great piles of chairs around, which didn't please Denny the Brock much. He's a pain in the neck when he wants to be. Jerry turned up an hour after the party started, looking really great. Bright red mini, big dangly earrings, tons of bangles. Know my mum wouldn't approve. I really fancy Jerry but of course Christian love is much deeper than just sexual love. The different strands of love all get mixed up together. I mean, God was willing to sacrifice his son for us which represents one kind of love. That's the kind of love that everything else stems from and might come over as the love for someone else at school. Another kind of love is the love you have for your parents. And then there's the sexual kind of love that you have in marriage. As far as sex before marriage is concerned, I think that it's a definite no, but that's for me and I wouldn't necessarily say that to everyone. I've sort of figured out how far I would go, but it's quite a difficult area.

Sometimes I'm totally appalled by Jerry. I mean, as we were dancing she said – straight out and casual as you like – 'Have you heard Mr Smythe has AIDS?' I couldn't believe it, and asked her how she knew. 'Well, you only have to look at him to know, don't you? He's gone all thin and pale, and is off all the time, and anyhow Jo says he's gay.' I nearly snubbed my nose on her mohican haircut in surprise. All those hairs up my nose made me sneeze. Luckily no snot came out – not that you'd notice, with what Jerry puts on her hair.

The party just went downhill. Don't know whether it was something Tony put in the drink, or that every-

one turned up drunk anyway. Jerry started pulling all the tablecloths off the tables. Some people thought the food would be better airborne, others were shaking up cans of beer and spraying people, somebody smashed a chair. A bunch of idiots started to try and take Mr Brock's trousers off, singing and shouting – a total bomb. Sometimes I despise my mates. They never seem to take care of anything around them. I mean, take all this stuff like the destruction of the ozone layer, the cutting down of the rain forests, people getting blown up in air crashes, killed on the roads in thousands and in train crashes. Gives me the impression that the world is wearing out and that it's not going to last for ever. I think it's all happening because we humans decided to go against God.

Look at what Jerry said, that Mr Smythe might be gay and have got AIDS. Being gay isn't God's way, but I have to admit it sometimes makes me feel ashamed of being a Christian when Tony goes on about that vicar who was gay and died of AIDS. Maybe it's hypocritical for Christians to preach about changing your lifestyle. Not that all Christians are the same. Charlie, who's a Christian but sex mad, says it's right on to sleep around as long as you wear a condom. And he thinks that being homosexual is all right because they're just born that way, and if God allows people to be born with those feelings, then it must be OK. I think if we all lived our lives in a really Christian way then the world would be a far better place. The trouble is that we live in a fallen world and AIDS is just part of that.

The thing about AIDS for me is, how do I react to someone who's got it? What happens if Mr Smythe comes back and teaches me, and he really has got AIDS? Do I risk getting close to him or stay right away? I am still figuring this one out. I've read that by touching or hugging the chance of getting AIDS is virtually zero. So that's fine. Not that I would ever hug Mr Smythe. But you do have to think about it. I mean, although I think at this moment that if I met someone with AIDS I'd behave normally, actually if the door opened now and in came Mr Smythe with AIDS, if I'm totally honest, I know I'd do a double take. There would be barriers between us, but I'd try and sort out what they are, and then try and overcome them and go up and talk to him and say 'Hi'. But I'd definitely be afraid of drinking out of the same cup as him, or using the same lavatory.

They try and teach us all about it at school. Sex education seems to be the fashion at the moment – except no one dares call it that. It's either 'growing up' or 'changes', 'personal growth studies' or 'social relationships', 'human reproduction' or 'human biology'. I can't understand why they can't call it 'sex' and have done with it. Personally I think God must know what sex is all about or he wouldn't have made us the way we are, nor would he have made it such fun, if I'm to believe what Tony says. Tony seems to think that because I'm a Christian it would be wrong for me to enjoy sex. It just shows how little people understand what it means to be a Christian. Sex is part of loving someone and being married to them. I bet when I get married I'll have just as much fun out of sex as Tony.

When I look at my friends at school who are rushing around going out with lots of different people, I don't see them as being particularly happy. Not that they often talk about it, and they don't seem to think much about the risk of AIDS. It's kind of hush-hush. But maybe no one talks to me because they know I'm a Christian.

It made me dead uncomfortable seeing them all touching one another up at the dance – without hiding anything. It's as if they're just trying to show off. Why can't they go and do it somewhere private? It's not as if the dance was meant to be a snogging competition.

Not that I'm feeling particularly saint-like at the moment. The party had its moments, but afterwards was a nightmare and I'm not sure I want to think about it just yet.

5 Jerry blows it

I hate Tony's guts. He thinks I've been screwing around with Miranda's friend Tom. I think he's jealous because I don't spend all my time with him. I like hanging around with Miranda and her lot at the college. Just thinking about all this makes me want a cigarette.

I've smoked for ages now and I'm not going to give up because I really enjoy it. I like a fag before I start eating. Otherwise I find I hurry my meal in order to have one at the end. But Dad doesn't like me smoking, particularly at breakfast, just as I don't like him eating all that eggs and bacon and stuff. I don't think killing animals is right. I thought about becoming vegetarian for three years, and now I have it upsets me seeing Dad eating meat. I started off not eating chicken and things because it seemed a bit mean. I still eat fish though. I suppose I think they're different because they live freely. Anyhow I'm not all that consistent about killing animals. I do wear leather shoes (I need a packet of 'odour-eaters' a week with canvas ones) and a leather jacket, and I sometimes give our cats real meat.

Yesterday I had to sit and watch Dad eating – not the best way of starting off the morning. I could see it was going to be a bad one anyway – the mood that Dad was in and the fact that I hadn't found a job yet. Dad wants me to do a typing course so that I can earn my own living. I'd rather travel. Mostly when he's getting at me I cope by walking off in a huff. He keeps bringing up all the bad things I've ever done since I was *three*, when I'm trying to argue about one specific thing. I suppose it's not entirely his fault. He thinks I'm wasting my life away. There's a generation gap in his views on all this. He's so up-tight, yet he can be a real sweetie. He says he's worked hard all his life so that I wouldn't have to be brought up in poverty. I was talking to him the other day about the dreams I have about my life and he just didn't get it.

I didn't like to say he's got a lot to learn but I do wish he'd try and see things from my angle.

Another thing is every time Dad comes back from work he's found a new course for me to do. I've got my own plans of working in a restaurant, learning to drive, playing in a band. Ever since I failed my GCSEs and left school it's been the same, and the discussions I have with Dad don't resolve anything. I always get things done at the last moment, but I'm quite confident that it's all going to get done in time. Dad isn't. He'll say, 'OK, if you have "got it all

together" – what have you done today?'

Not much yesterday, I've got to grant him. I got up late, sat around, thought about what I was going to do, which wasn't much – except go to the school party. It was funny going back there. Luckily they needed me to play the sax in the band, so I didn't have to pay for a ticket. Also, I wanted to make it up with Tony. I know he's bad for me but I can't do without him. As for Dad, he'd expected me to go down to the library, again, and then go on and see the Careers Officer.

What I would like to happen, ideally, is for Dad to be able to see two years ahead, when I've sorted out my life, because I've really got the confidence that I will. When he got back from work, he started on at me and I thought, 'Oh no – not again' and I switched off from what he was saying. He got annoyed but still went on and on. I'm sure I will get it together – at least, that's what I keep telling myself. Parents should have faith.

I didn't know how it would turn out last night. I was feeling a bit frustrated when I arrived and thought maybe I'd look round a bit and see what I could pick up if Tony was still being foul. Apart from Tony, I haven't had much sex in the last year or so, but when I have, I've made them use a condom. People say that condoms are so unromantic – and they are. There's always that hitch in the middle when one of you has to say something about it. I know the dangers – it's not just AIDS and other diseases, but getting pregnant as well. I do worry about it but I don't go out of my way to read all the junk we're told to. It all seems to say the same thing.

Some of my friends started having sex when they were fifteen or sixteen – one or two earlier – but most haven't had it yet. It's funny, at school there's always someone who wins the 'Miss Slag of the Year' award. A couple of years ago, they probably said it was me. But *my* reputation comes as much from flirting and showing myself to be sexually active as from actually sleeping around.

Until AIDS came along, I didn't personally think much about the possibility of getting any sexually transmitted diseases. And knowing about AIDS has stopped some of my friends from sleeping around as well (though not all of them). I've heard it has changed the habits of the gay population and students, so that they screw around less. There's a risk to riding your bicycle, or flying in an aeroplane, or crossing the road, and you don't have too much control over those. With AIDS you *do* have some control over the risk, and quite easily too.

I know I'm not Tony's only girl, though I hate it when he flaunts other ones at me, like last night with Rachel. I don't know why there seems to be more need for men to show off conquests than there is with us.

Dad was in a right rage about me going out. It upsets him when I leave to go somewhere and we're both still angry, but it's not fair to lay all that on me when I'm trying to enjoy myself. He worries about the parties I go to and thinks that someone will come and inject me with a drug or something. You know, like people walk around with a loaded syringe of heroin and pop it into your arm while you're dancing. Parents are utterly and completely mad sometimes. I've never known anyone try to push heroin at parties because you never know who's going to be there. All that happened tonight was a lot of stupid fifth-formers throwing food around.

The only time I've been offered the stuff was on a bus on the way home one night about a year ago, and I thought it was a joke. This scraggly casual type sat down on the seat next to me. I thought he was trying to pick me up, but he just said, "Ere, do ya want some "H"?' and I said 'No' and that was it.

There's one ex-friend I know who uses it – but he's not a friend any more because you can't have a conversation with him. His face is grey for a start. He stares into the sky when you're talking to him and he only understands what you're saying about five minutes later. He got into a bad scene with drugs when doing props in a theatre. He's into stealing now – video equipment and stuff. I'm sure he'll get put away one day and I don't see it as much of a loss. He isn't a personality any more.

Anyhow, to get back to the school party. Tony was getting everybody drunk out of their tiny minds with his so-called 'Gargleblaster'. Not me – once bitten twice shy, as my mum used to say. In the past, when I was into Goth and dressing in black all the time, I'd have used a bit of dope instead, to help me groove when I was playing. But just recently I heard that dope destroys your brain cells, makes you forget things up to six weeks after having the last puff. Tony says that's rubbish (though it could be why he did so badly in his GCSEs). A friend of Dad's showed me a photocopy of this piece from a medical magazine. I don't want to go popping off *my* brain cells, thanks very much. I've only got one set and they'll have to do me. So although I did have a leaf or two of my home-grown with me, I wasn't going to use it even if I did feel right down.

I was clasped together with Steve in a smoochy dance which was making me feel horny, and we were talking – of all things – about the ozone layer! It did seem a rather unromantic thing to be discussing – but was typical of my discussions with Steve. I told him that as soon as I heard about the problems, I started getting ozone-friendly stuff. I actually went into a shop once and bought a thing of fly-spray costing £2.30. When I came out, I found it wasn't ozone-friendly and threw it away. I felt really good

until I went back in again and found that the ozone-friendly spray was only 85p. Steve fell about laughing and I quite lost my sexy mood.

Mind you, I don't go out of my way to support those issues generally, like animal rights or saving the whales, but if someone has a petition in town I sign it. Steve said I should be more supportive of those kinds of issues but I can't be bothered. I told him that if someone came to me and said, 'Listen – we know you're interested in animal rights. Come and break into this laboratory and rescue some,' then I'd probably do it. I'd feel radical doing that, but to actually go out and make some effort myself – I just don't have the energy.

I talked to Miranda about it last week when I was deciding whether I'd go and learn typing at the CFE (to please Dad). She said she'd rather they didn't experiment on animals at all because there are other ways. But if they found a new drug that might save people with AIDS or leukaemia, or *her* baby, then she would want them to test it on a rabbit first, and she might even give them her pet rabbit!

Me, when I think of people using animals to experiment with shampoos and cigarettes – then it shouldn't be allowed. I have a choice over smoking. I know the dangers and I take the risk – it's up to me. But I don't see why animals should suffer just because we choose to do something we know harms us.

Between sexy blasts, I had to go and have an argument with David. I just told him why I thought Mr Smythe wasn't around. I mean, everyone knows. I don't know why David's so hung up about it. Later, when I was with him on the way home, I suddenly realized there *is* something that gets me worked up – the rich being so greedy. I think greed is the main problem at the moment, we're using the world up. And the rich are getting richer and the poor are getting poorer, it's like going back to the Victorians – like *Upstairs and Downstairs* on telly. I don't see any way out.

When the police picked us up – just for enjoying ourselves – I thought, 'England's just like America – owned by cops who are all government agents.' I definitely want to go somewhere better. I felt worse for David than I did for me when they found those leaves. He's so innocent. Why did I have to involve him? I'm no good for anybody.

Dad and I didn't say anything in the car on the way home. I'd confirmed his worst fears now. As I was going to bed, he came up and said, 'Look, let's discuss all this in the morning. I know you're tired and have had a bad time. There's no point in going over it all now.' Good old Dad. I saw it was 3 a.m. and faded into sleep.

6 Miranda stays away

Rach brought my shoes round this morning before school, bit the worse for wear – like Rach. She had tried to do her best but they still smelled of sick. Tony and Rachel – can't believe it. I mean, Tony's poison. Wouldn't wish my worst enemy to be touched by that snake. I know I used to go out with him – but I never slept with him. I asked Rachel if she'd gone mad or something. She needs her head examining. She may be taking 'A's and thinking of going to university, but this doesn't give her any credits towards having common sense. I'm glad I wasn't at the party, and even more glad I've left all that scene behind. I've got to give Rach some credit though – not letting him touch her up. It's lucky they don't think you can get AIDS from just kissing.

People amaze me – they think it's never going to happen to them. From what I've picked up from Mum, with all her experience in this area, I don't think people in general have been properly affected by the news of AIDS. That's one of the most worrying things. I don't think they've got a clue. I don't know how many people it's going to reach – but there'll always be some who go on behaving as if there's no tomorrow. The television programmes and advertisements or whatever never really hit what it's all about. It's not just a question of taking precautions to avoid getting it, like wearing a condom or using a clean needle. It's deeper than that. They need to encourage people to change the way they behave – not sleep around or take drugs.

One very tricky problem for the government must be deciding whether they should give clean needles to drug addicts, which would prevent them from getting AIDS but might encourage them to use drugs.

Rachel had more important things on her mind. Sue was in floods of tears at the party because Jerry was flirting with Paul. Absolutely not on – but I can't understand Sue being so upset. She and Paul have been together for ages – they're like a boring old married couple. Paul would never have the guts to go off with Jerry – she's far too dangerous for him. Still, I do sympathize with Sue. You can never completely understand what's going on inside other people. Sometimes you just have to trust.

Discussed with Rachel how difficult it is getting to know someone well. I remember all the things I revealed to Tony in the past that I wouldn't tell anyone else. It made me feel really vulnerable. Each day I was thinking will it go on? Will I still be able to talk to him in the same way? Is he telling what I feel to all his mates? And he was – the bastard. Not only that, but he was making up a whole lot of stuff as well – about how he had slept with me, how much in love with him I was, and how he was teaching me to be a wonderful lover.

Reckon old Rach must have been drunk – losing her inhibitions like that. I told her how stupid she'd been going anywhere near him sober, let alone drunk. Being plastered does definitely make it more difficult to say 'no', even if it does help release some other inhibitions.

Can't talk to any grown-up nowadays without them saying, 'Remember, it's your body – you can say "no".' I know it's my body and the worry about AIDS won't stop me from sleeping with someone if I want to. I'll just always take the right precautions

– not just against AIDS, but against other diseases, and there's no way I'm going to get pregnant before I get married. A bloke is just going to have to use a condom whether he likes it or not, otherwise I won't go with him. And I wouldn't choose anyone at risk. I'd just say who else have you slept with? What kind of people were they? Is there any chance you've got AIDS? I've only one life and I intend to keep it – romance or no romance.

Not sure Rachel wasn't still drunk – her mouth was so loose today. Not like her at all – she's usually so discreet. It turns out that Jerry had hinted that there had been something all wrong with her upbringing. An uncle used to come and tuck her up in bed when she was about seven. He used to touch her under the bedclothes and make her play with his willie, and promise never, ever to tell anyone about it – or he'd go to jail.

I suppose we've all had some experience like that. I remember I was out walking in the park last April Fools' Day with a friend, and it was a really misty morning. We were followed by this man who was in the bushes, and we heard this shuffling behind us on the gravel. We looked round and there he was, with his trousers round his knees and his willie sticking out. I forgot to feel frightened because my friend was so terrified. I ended up being really brave and turning round and shouting at him to go away. You always think of something clever to say afterwards like,

'Gosh – even my cat's got a bigger one and he's been done.' My mum said when she was flashed at, she just shouted, 'I'm not impressed. I see twenty like that every day.' I said he probably thought she was a prostitute, rather than a nurse.

It might be good just to laugh at them – because that would be really humiliating. Another friend told me that it happened to her in one of those Southern Railway trains where you're in a compartment without a corridor. It was actually very frightening because she couldn't get out. He'd put his hand on her knee – and she had just laughed, even though he'd called her a 'frigid bitch'. She didn't know why she laughed, because it could have been quite dangerous. It was probably just nerves. Luckily nothing actually happened.

Leroy, my brother, said that if he'd been there he'd have punched him, but only if he'd been small. I asked him if he was talking about the guy's willie or his height.

Rachel was all upset and wondered why no one had ever flashed *her*. Was she that unfanciable? I think it was a sign of her tiredness. She looked completely washed-out – I don't know how she'll survive today. I told her another few minutes last night and she'd have seen Tony's willie. Mum gave her a couple of aspirin and some to take with her. Rach said she'd come round this evening if she hadn't overdosed on aspirin.

7 The consequences for David

I had never been in a police station before. My first thought was, 'How on earth am I going to tell my parents?' They'll never trust me again. They'll never be convinced that I wasn't taking drugs. Being pulled in by the police made me *feel* guilty even though I know I never touch a thing.

This is what happened. As usual, it turned out to be Tony's fault for lacing the punch, but as usual he was nowhere to be seen – and certainly not down at the cop shop. Jerry and I had left the party after clearing up (yes – me again, good little me, martyred little me). We were feeling fantastic – I'm sure it was the alcohol – and we were arsing around, with Mark and Sophy from the fifth year. We were walking along the tops of cars, moving bikes from one place to another, lying in the middle of the road pretending to be dead – pretty innocent stuff on the whole. Suddenly one of the passing cars stopped. Large boots materialized, on a ten-foot tall, bearded, SAS-type police officer. It wasn't my whole short life but the image of my parents and what they were going to say that flashed instantly through my mind. I sobered

up in 0.001 seconds flat when this voice said, 'Excuse me, sir, are you trying to be sleeping policemen?'

My first encounter with the law, which was definitely out to intimidate us. Not too difficult to do either. We had the two girls with us still, not that that made any difference. The policeman and his sidekick started questioning us. They must have noticed we were jittery, so they asked us to turn out our pockets. I just had some old bus tickets and two buttons. Jerry brought out a little clear packet with a couple of what looked like ordinary plant leaves. The policeman looked at it and said to her, 'Right, you're nicked.' Then he said to all of us, 'Put your hands on the car, and spread your legs.' Real Cagney and Lacey stuff, like being on TV. I thought of praying but didn't like calling on God's help just because I was in trouble. Then I thought of doing a bunk but realized it would only add to my problems being rugby tackled by this ape. After they'd searched us all, the gorilla got his walkie-talkie out and called some back-up in. Another police car came along and they decided to take us all down to the police station. I went in the first car with Jerry. We were sitting in the back and they made us put our hands up. Suddenly it was no longer fun but serious. I said something stupid like, 'What do you think I'm going to do, throw all my heroin out of the window?' and got the reply, 'Don't you be cheeky'. So I kept my hands up and they drove us to the station.

CUSTODY RECORD

Police Station

Station reference

Reasons for Arrest

Suspicion of
Possession of
Drugs of controlled

(Mr. Mrs. Miss Maj)

Surname JONES

First Names DAVID

Grounds for Detention

To obtain
evidence
substance

Address S. Colliers Wood

Occupation Schoolboy

A notice setting out my rights has been read to me and I have been provided with a copy.

Age 17

Place of Birth London

Height

D.O.B. 16.9.15

Signature of person detained ✓

Time

Date

† I want a solicitor as soon as practicable

Signature of person detained

Time/Date contacted

† I do not want a solicitor at this time

Signature of person detained

Time

Date

At the time of service of Notice - notification of detention to named person
*requested/not requested.

†Named Person Juvenile - Mother
Called to Station

Time 00.15

Arrested by:

Name P.C. 1247 JONES

Rank P.C. No 1247

Place of Arrest

Sex M

RECORD OF *PRISONER/DETAINED PERSON'S PERSONAL PROPERTY

Name ..... H.S. H.bork .... C003.

Searched at .... Reason for removal of personal property from prisoner must be stated on Custody Log

Signature(s) of Officer(s) Searching .... hrs. on .... Rank ...... H.S. No. H.D. Station ..... New Road

1 CASH - in figures £   5.79   PC.124. D. Hodge
  and words   Give pounds 79p

2	Glasswallet	11	Name ... HODGSON .... Rank and Number ...12.4.2.
3	Hankies	12	
4	Matches	13	
5	Handketch	14	
6	Belt	15	
7	Shoes	16	
8		17	
9		18	
10		19	
		20	

I have retained items numbered .... at my own risk and the above is a true record of my property ....

The following remain unsealed, Item No.s .... item| At .... hrs. on ....

At .... hrs. on .... bagged and sealed with Seal No. ....

Nos. .... By .... Name & Rank ....

interfere with evidence/assist escape/valuables/evidence relating to case.

By .... were removed from prisoner, to prevent damage/injury/will .... and are in the care of the Custody Officer.

* Delete as appropriate   † Record Action on Log

Name .... Rank & No. .... Signature. .... Signed .... Date all the remaining items were

.... Signature.

PAC 41 (7/87)

We had to fill out a million forms. They were treating us like criminals, and although I hadn't done anything really wrong, I knew I wasn't totally in the right. They took Jerry away because she was the one who had had the drugs, and she had to put all her possessions in a little plastic bag. They lined the rest of us up along a wall at the back of the room and interrogated us for about ten minutes, not telling us what was happening or whether we were allowed a lawyer. Then they brought Jerry back and started asking her where she got her marijuana leaves from.

Finally they said, 'We'll have to search you all,' and I was really frightened. Sophy was hysterical, laughing and crying and saying she wanted her parents. She calmed down when they arrived. Not that her parents looked particularly calm – more like pressure cookers about to release. By this time they'd contacted all our parents and we were taken into a room one by one, searched, and brought back. We had to take absolutely everything off – it was totally humiliating. I had to stand naked in the middle of the room while a policeman walked round me once then said, 'OK, now we'll search through your possessions.' This was all in front of Mum and Dad. I felt completely shocked and didn't know which way to look. We were there for about three hours altogether.

The police kept emphasizing we were in big trouble, and the one who picked us up was being really nasty. He wanted the names of all the people at the party but I didn't give them. I was very confused over what to do – thinking should I lie or should I tell the truth? In the end, I didn't quite tell the whole truth, but didn't quite lie either. Finally, they let all of us go except Jerry.

I was taken apart by Dad on the way home. 'What do you think you were doing?' 'Haven't we brought you up right?' 'What do you expect if you associate with that sort of girl?' 'Why can't you be more like your brother? He never gets into this kind of trouble.' 'There'll be no allowance for you for the next month.' But what was worse was Mum just sitting there, looking even more accusing than the policeman. I wished I was dead.

8 The fuzz teach Tony

Can't remember how I got into bed. It seemed to be
my own. I definitely hadn't been in it long enough
when there was a crashing at the front door. I yelled
to Mum to get it. Fortunately, as it turned out, she'd
already gone. I wasn't going to answer it myself, but
it began to sound as if it was being broken in.

Two policemen in full uniform and me in just my
none too clean Y-fronts made a great sight for Mrs

Jones staring out from behind her curtains opposite. I didn't feel in a particularly advantageous position. They asked me if I was Tony Jacobs of 16 Honeywell Street. Well, this was it folks. They could bloody well see I was, couldn't they? What did they want me to do? Show them my name tape in my pants?

We ended up at the police station with them getting heavy. Luckily, as I'm over seventeen, they didn't ask Mum to come too. She'd have really freaked. I didn't know it then, but it turned out half the school had been down there in the last few hours. All because of that bloody fool Jerry carrying her home-grown stuff around.

They explained my rights and then two of them took turns in questioning me. They immediately started saying they knew who I got my drugs from; the names of the people I supplied; the kinds of drugs I supplied them with. They got me totally confused, put words into my mouth, went over things again and again so that I began contradicting myself. They were not saying anything definite about why they had picked me up, except that they had had their eye on me for some time. I sweated and sweated but didn't tell them anything – just went on and on saying 'no'. I gradually realized that it was all to do with the school party. Nothing to do with Adrian's, or the one Jack took me to. I was glad I'd kept silent.

It wasn't over yet, however, because having given me the third degree, they then got into the earnest 'this is for your own good, son' lecture mode. They were spelling out the links between drugs and AIDS. They said that in Edinburgh – one of the drug centres in the UK – half of all drug users are HIV positive, and most of them had begun to use injectable drugs at about my age.

I told them there wasn't a problem. They could solve it all by supplying drug users with clean needles and syringes. One of them agreed it might help, but said it wasn't going to make the problem go away. Another effect is that as many prostitutes are drug users AIDS is spreading more and more to heterosexuals. He explained, somewhat needlessly, that 'heterosexual' means a woman having sex with a man (rather than 'homosexual' which means a man having sex with another man, or a woman having sex with another woman). I knew all that – but what I didn't know was that a woman can't normally get AIDS by making love with another woman. I knew women get AIDS – but I didn't know that one in three intravenous drug users are women and that if they have AIDS and then get pregnant, their babies have at least a one in two chance of dying from AIDS too. I didn't expect the fuzz to be so clued up about all this. Maybe they have their uses after all.

I finally left after being there two hours. I was totally wiped out – and I'm going to get Jerry for being such a stupid bitch.

Mum freaked out totally when I told her. Think

she felt guilty not having my dad around to help control me. Waste of bloody time that would be. He's the kind of dad who phones a week after my birthday and says, 'Happy birthday. Congratulations making it to fifteen,' and I have to say, 'Actually, Dad, I'm sixteen and my birthday was last week.'

The thing that hurt most was when I did try and resurrect my relationship with him. Before that, I'd phone him up occasionally to say, 'Hi, Dad – how are you doing?' and all I'd get back was a long wrinkly diatribe about how badly I was doing at school. I'd always get negative vibes from the other end of the phone so I kept hanging up on him. I want him to accept me for what I am. But one time I remember ringing him up and pouring out my heart to him, saying how all my life I had thought about this fab father who would have played football with me in the garden and flown kites with me on Sunday. I ended up by saying that he was a real shit and I didn't like him at all. I got it all off my chest and we finished up having a serious chat. He said, 'OK, let's start this friendship again. I'll phone you every week.' That was a year ago and I haven't heard from him since.

9 The regrets of Rachel

David and Jerry. I just can't believe it. Jerry well, I mean, maybe – but David never. As soon as I got to school I looked around for Tony. Not sure whether I did or didn't want to talk to him, but I did want him to know I was there. It seemed as if there was some unfinished business between us. Every time the door opened during registration I stared round to see if it was him. Talking to Miranda had made me feel that I'd done the right thing, but it hadn't taken the ache away. There's still something in me that's attracted to that shit. Anyway – no Tony all day.

The school were furious about the party but luckily they didn't get too heavy. They talked to a group of us and said that they might have to take disciplinary action, like no more parties involving alcohol. I suppose if they had expelled us all, there wouldn't have been much of the lower sixth left.

Jerry came into school to pick up her sax. She looked even worse than I felt. If she gets done for drugs it'll put an end to her travelling. I told her that I really hope she gets off and that I couldn't believe the police would be hard on her for having a couple of leaves. (Not that I would know though.) She was really cool with me. I suppose I'll have to live with that. Though for me there was a good side to going off with Tony, which seems strange given that the action is usually where that shit is.

And where the hell was he? I just couldn't concentrate all day – a mixture of missing Tony and being totally wiped out. Whatever did Tony do after copping out of Adrian's party and leaving me high and dry? I even considered ringing him from the school phone, but pulled out in time. My ex-gargleblasted mind exploded with, 'What the hell do you think you are doing, Rachel Packsworth? This guy's a walking graveyard who stands you up at a party, so that you have to walk home alone and risk getting raped by a garden gnome, and you want to *ring* him?' I began hoping he was down at the police station being third-degreed for possession of drugs. It would serve him bloody well right.

The trouble is, Steve's giving me the cold shoulder today, instead of the 'cry on' one. I'm beginning to think no one loves me any more. I've managed to lose all my friends in one night.

The whole school is in total disarray. No one can believe that David's mixed up in it. The teachers all think it was Jerry who led him on. I think David's enjoying his new image – having a slightly tarnished halo has given him a lot of street cred. Maybe God forgot him for a while last night.

Accusations were flying around. We had a long lecture at assembly about how the school was getting a very bad name. Certain people at the party had been found to be in possession of drugs and that would not be tolerated. Mr Brock stood by the head's side looking like a smug sergeant major with an 'I knew it would come to this' expression on his face. By the end of the platform harangue I think everybody felt personally responsible for the whole fiasco.

Not that I was in the clear. I was in deep trouble from Mum over the tear in her dress. I promised I'd sew it up so she wouldn't notice. I'll have to borrow Miranda's machine after school and get her to help me. She's a whizz at dressmaking. I wish she was still at school. I miss her, and her commonsense-type

advice being immediately available in this kind of crisis. Steve kept glancing over at me. God, it's bad enough to do something really crass like leaving with Tony last night – but to have accusing looks from Steve this morning as well is almost more than I can stand. Why can't people just leave me alone?

David then came up at lunch-time to say that Jerry had told him that Mr Smythe was away because he'd got AIDS. I told him that was rubbish and that I thought it was cancer. The way rumours get around this place is disgusting. I put my foot in it later though – or in this case my whole leg. I was talking to

David's older brother Jim on the bus on the way home. I was telling him what Jerry had said about Mr Smythe (I'm as bad a muck spreader as everyone else — if not worse), and saying that I didn't understand the real difference between being HIV positive and having AIDS. Being another health freak, like his friend Pete, he explained that HIV stands for Human Immunodeficiency Virus and that being 'positive' for the virus means that there are antibodies against the virus circulating around in your blood. Unfortunately, unlike other antibodies, they don't stop you from getting the disease. The virus attacks the immune system straight away but you only say someone has AIDS (or Acquired Immune Deficiency Syndrome) when the person actually gets ill. This happens when their immune system is so knocked off that they get all sorts of infections and illnesses.

Slack-tongued me then had to say that I thought AIDS was just a homosexual problem, and if homosexuals changed the way they lived, it wouldn't be a problem for anyone any more. I'd put my mouth into gear before my mind, as it suddenly occurred to me that Jim might be gay. He certainly knows a lot about the subject and lectured me all the way home about people who blame AIDS on gays.

In the end, I couldn't decide whether Jim was gay or just didn't like minorities being got at for what they are. He said he couldn't understand people who thought it served gays right if they got AIDS. And

In the UK, by the end of 1989, 11,218 people had tested positive for the AIDS virus, of whom 1,388 have died and 2,649 have signs of the AIDS disease. Of these 2,649, 82 per cent caught the virus from homosexual or bisexual contacts, 8 per cent from blood transfusions, 5 per cent from heterosexual contacts, 4 per cent from intravenous drug use, and 1 per cent were children of HIV positive mothers. However, more and more of the new cases appearing now are intravenous drug users, and there has also been a small rise in the numbers getting AIDS from heterosexual contacts. In the whole world, by October 1989, 182,463 cases of people with the AIDS disease had been reported, but the true number was estimated as being close to half a million.

In America there has been a move to test immigrants to the country for HIV. However, the figures suggest that infected Americans are effectively exporting the virus to everyone else. Of all the people known to have AIDS in the world: 66 per cent are in the Americas, 18 per cent in Africa, 14 per cent in Europe, 1 per cent in Asia, and 1 per cent in Australia and New Zealand.

that people in America who had AIDS and gave blood knowing it was infected were scum. He said the problem in the States is that people get paid for giving blood. So druggies often sell their blood to get money for a fix and this is how so many people with haemophilia got AIDS. He thinks the poor haemophiliacs got the worst deal. They are born with something missing from their blood (factor viii) and need to have regular injections of factor viii to stop them bleeding and bruising very easily. The factor viii had sometimes been made from infected blood and so the AIDS virus got passed on to lots of haemophiliacs. This was before they knew how to test for the AIDS virus. The factor viii they use now is OK, but a lot of people were already infected and they had then passed it on to their wives, who in turn passed it on to their babies.

Jim said there are lots of myths about AIDS which have to be destroyed. Like that you can get it just from living in the same house as someone with the disease, from toilet seats or door handles; from swim-

ming pools or headlice; from kissing or holding hands; or sharing cups and glasses, or eating off the same plate. (David will be glad you can't get it from taking communion.)

As far as these risks and me is concerned, I'm glad
nothing happened last night. I think you have to be
in a serious relationship to have sexual intercourse
with the opposite sex because of the risks involved –
it's not worth it otherwise. Unlike what Tony was
saying the other day: 'Sure, sexually transmitted diseases are something to be scared of, but this shouldn't
stop you from doing what comes naturally.' He just
treats them as if they are one of life's little nasties

which can be avoided. He says it's bad luck if you catch them, and after all, you could get snuffed out at any time – it's just one of those things.

My trouble is that as soon as someone starts being interested in me – like Steve – I go off them. I fall for the ones who aren't interested in me. Or I go for someone really dodgy like Tony, who I know I shouldn't touch with a barge pole because even the barge pole would catch something nasty.

I had tea with Miranda. Her mum thinks the fuss at school is all a bit of a storm in a teacup. I wish my mum was like her. Some of the people named hadn't even been at the party. The police must have thought they were on to something big. But I suppose you can't really blame them for that.

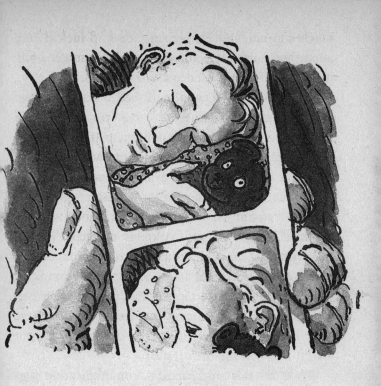

10 *The torments of Steve*

It should really be my parents telling this part of the
story. It was not much fun for me – but a real shock
horror for them. They sent me to a school where
they thought I'd get a 'broad' education and become
streetwise – but I don't think they reckoned on this.

My motor-mouth sister informed me that Dad had
come home after work to find Mum in hysterics.

David's mum had rung to ask her if she'd heard about the party last night. David (that arsehole of *all* people!) had got picked up by the police at 1 a.m., when I was safely tucked up in bed with my faithful (I hope) teddy bear. The prick was lying in the road pretending to be a sleeping policeman – ha, ha. Even the 'churchies' have to let it all out sometime. Jerry was with him and had her 'roll your own' kit, along with a couple of leaves from her 'home grown' – wouldn't ya know. She's such a fool.

David's mum wanted to know whether I'd been involved. Of course Mum immediately assumed I had been. Why do parents have so little faith? Smoking ganja is not one of the vices I find even faintly attractive, and anyhow dancing on people's cars in the early hours of the morning can be dangerous to your health and bad for the cars.

While all this interparental communication was going on I was cycling back from school – without a care in the world, except for Rachel and all the speculation about Jerry and David. I wouldn't have recognized Rachel as the same human being. Last night she looked absolutely fab in all her war-paint. Today she looked bomb blasted. Dead from the top neurone downwards – a real Beauty into the Beast story. I couldn't help being aware of her though my feelings are pretty mixed up and include a fair bit of deep utter green jealousy.

I was riding my ace Italian racer, bought off Bob

(somebody Tony introduced me to – he probably took a rake-off). I'd only had it a couple of months. It's a smashing bike and cost me 150 quid. A real snip – or so I thought: 743 frame, racing wheels, twelve gears, and high tech quick release clips. Lost in these reveries, I almost ran head-on into the open door of a white van with someone standing by it. I slammed on my brakes and turned on a well-practised stream of observations on the driver's lack of respectable parentage. It was a police van!!!

''Scuse me, sir', said this very polite voice. 'Is that your bicycle that you're riding?' Christ, I thought, is that all? The school had been abuzz with nothing else except how we were all going to get hauled in because Jerry had been found 'in possession'. I just couldn't stop my mind turning into my mouth. 'Oh, is that all? You mean it's not about . . . ?' 'About what would that be, sir?' My mind fell instantly and coldly back under my control again. 'Er – I mean about my bike – yes, it's mine. Why?' 'We have reason to believe it's stolen, sir and it's my duty to arrest you and tell you that anything you say may be taken down in evidence . . .' I knew the rest. I watched TV too. I'd have a police record, I'd never be able to go to America, there'd be a whole range of jobs I wouldn't be able to apply for. 'Would you mind accompanying me down to the station, please, sir?' Here I was dissolving into a puddle of panic and embarrassed shame, wanting only to be washed away down a drain in the road, and he was calling me 'sir'. I held out my wrists for the handcuffs, but he said that wouldn't be necessary.

In the 'stolen goods' room down at the station there were pictures of my bike plastered over every wall. It was worth a thousand quid (I knew I had an eye for bikes), and had been stolen off the back of some Italian's Porsche four months ago. The poor guy had come over to do a cycling tour in Scotland and had had his bike stolen the first day here. Maybe I'll get a reward – better still, maybe I'll get Bob.

While I was sitting there dead miserable, the police rang my parents. 'Could you come down to the police station, please? We've just arrested your son and he's asked that you be present when we question him.' 'But, but, but . . .' I tried to get out, 'please tell them it's about my bike and nothing else.' Too late, the damage was done and they'd already rung off.

What a day. First Jerry and David, then Rachel, then this. I tried turning my mind to other things to squeeze out the huge floods of anxiety freezing my brain. I looked in my rucksack and found a heavy questionnaire on the favourite subject at school at the moment – AIDS. My performance had showed me to be dead ignorant, so I stared at some of the answers to pass the time till my parents came.

– ear piercing and tattoos. You can catch AIDS from the needles they use. If you have these things done, make sure that the person doing them uses sterilized needles.

– what kills the virus? It is a really weedy virus outside the body and can get knocked off by soap, disinfectants and heat.

– can you get it from door knobs, lavatory seats, plates, glasses, swimming pools and from holding hands? This one didn't worry me – I know you can't get it any of these ways – but there are about thirteen people in school who are going to have a hard time in life wiping lav seats and door knobs because they think you can. Pete, who'd danced with Jerry last night, thinks you can get it from holding hands and is now convinced that he's got infected from her – what a dick. You can't get it from coughing or sneezing, and there's no evidence at the moment that you can get it from 'french' kissing (just as well – though I don't think I'd fancy a slobbery kiss from someone with AIDS!)

– how not to get AIDS and have a great sex life. It's beginning to sound as if sticking with wanking or using inch-thick condoms might be the only safeguard. Don't fancy either of these for the rest of my life. Actually, if you take good care – don't sleep around, don't inject drugs, and use condoms when you don't know what your partner may have been up to – then you're going to be completely safe.

At this point my thoughts were interrupted by my parents' arrival. They were both as white as sheets. Mum couldn't say anything as she was in tears, Dad was tight-lipped but managed to say 'Hello'. 'Look,' I said, 'before you say anything – I've been arrested because they think that bike I bought off Bob was stolen.' Some colour came back into their faces. 'Oh, is that all? We thought it was about . . .'

I don't know if it was relief at seeing them, but I suddenly felt as if I was going to faint.

11 Sex or sax for Jerry

Hated myself for getting drunk last night. Don't know why I told Rachel what happened with my uncle. There are some things I'd vowed I'd never tell anybody. I'd always thought of Rachel as a good friend, but the way she sneaked off with Tony last night was a real betrayal. She's bound to tell him, or someone else, and I don't want other people knowing all about me.

I collected my sax from school but I didn't see Tony. I wonder why he hasn't rung me today? He can be terrific, but most of the time he's a real bastard. When we argue sometimes I know I'm wrong, so I admit it and say I'm sorry, but he can't even admit the possibility that he may be wrong, let alone say 'sorry'. I mean, everyone has to be wrong some time so might as well admit it. I don't feel I lose anything by saying 'I'm sorry', even if I have to make a joke of it in order to save my ego. Usually I even mean it, though sometimes I say it in a way that suggests I'm not really sorry at all. When I do that to Tony, it makes him mad.

Saying sorry to Dad last night – or rather, this morning – was no problem. I definitely meant it – after everything I'd put him through. For once he was really great. Didn't blink an eyelid. Just said, 'OK, if you're sorry, and know what you've done wrong, it's good enough for me.' I gave him a hug when he came in from work and went upstairs to blast away on my sax. This always makes me feel better.

What really used to make me feel good was the evenings when we played in the band. Everybody just met and got on with it. Music is important to me because it's a universal language and all that. Even if you're not musical, you can listen to music that you like. What expresses my music best is jazz. If you're playing classical music it's like most of the expression is the composer's, but with jazz most of

it is your own to do what you want with. I nearly
gave up playing before I got really into it. First it was
having to wear a brace, which didn't help with a
saxophone. Then it was my friends walking past the
house hearing me practise and taking the piss.

What with playing the sax and staying up all night
I have this problem about getting up at four o'clock

in the afternoon. I love sunlight and hate missing it. It's just that the wonderful conversations which start in the early evening and go on until four o'clock in the morning don't help. But apart from the sunlight, the mornings aren't all that important at the moment. I haven't much to do during the day, so I'd rather lie in in the mornings and enjoy the evenings. Although me lying in all day gets under Dad's skin, at least now he's there for me when I'm miserable. Like last week when I'd quarrelled with Tony, or today when I'm in deep shit with the police.

He's sure changed from last year when I was in trouble. One time I was found out for skiving off school. What I wanted him to say was, 'Never mind, I still love you.' But instead he said, 'Why are you looking so miserable? Are you on hard drugs?' I'd just come downstairs from having a good cry on my own and my eyes were all red, so it wasn't what I really wanted to hear. I still want a reassuring hug now and again, but when he gets irritated with me, it's more a question of me hugging him.

It's taken me a long time to realize that grown-ups have problems too. When I had an argument with Dad the other day I went round to Miranda's house and I was all weepy, and everyone there said, 'Oh, he was probably just in a bad mood, or had had a bad day in the office.' The argument was all because he'd said, 'Please do the washing-up before you go out today.' I went out, saw the Careers Officer, and dropped in at the library. I was feeling so good that I cooked supper and got Dad some beer. But all he said when he came home was, 'Why haven't you done the washing-up?' I had just forgotten, that was all – but why didn't he notice all the other things I had done? When I'd calmed down a bit I thought, well, he did ask me to wash up, after all.

I really like Miranda's mum. Sometimes I feel quite cosy with just Dad and me at home – but I also miss Mum, like there was a great big piece of life missing. I try not to think too much about it – what's the point now she's dead? It won't bring her back. I've sort of adopted Miranda's mum instead. She's really down to earth and you can say anything to her. (Well, almost anything. I wouldn't tell her about how I used to smoke dope. She wouldn't like that – she'd think it was stupid.)

She doesn't judge people. Like she's looking after the AIDS patients up at the hospital, but she accepts them as people first. She says you can't write anyone off, though she believes in following what the Bible says about no sex before marriage, or outside marriage, and no homosexual sex, and she wouldn't put herself at risk of AIDS. She thinks that people who get AIDS nowadays probably knew that they were putting themselves at risk, but she doesn't really see it as being their own fault. She says to them, 'Well, you knew the risks because you've seen the television programmes and people are talking about it a lot now, but you still go out and share a needle with your druggy friend, or sleep with your girlfriend who you know has slept with a guy who has AIDS.' She helps them, but she can't really sympathize.

The sad part is that when she saw them first they had just come up for a blood test and looked perfectly well. If they were found to be HIV positive, and therefore had the virus in their body, they usually stayed OK for several months – sometimes even years. But they had to be warned not to have sex or give blood because at the time when they were feeling perfectly well they were just as likely to pass it on as when they became ill. Her job was to explain to AIDS patients that what the virus does is damage their body's ability to fight infections and cancers. As this happens, they start to get illnesses more often. The early changes doctors look for are swelling of the glands in the neck, under the arms, and in the groin; sweating, increasing tiredness, and repeated infections.

When Miranda's mum said this, Miranda and I immediately thought we must have the dreaded lurgy. It all seemed to be the kind of thing we suffered from the whole time. Miranda's mum laughed and said, 'Don't go and craze yourself, you two. You've not got AIDS every time you've got enlarged glands and a sore throat. Many, many other things can cause these. You'd know if you'd put yourselves at risk of getting AIDS. The best thing you could do then is go and get a blood test. A family doctor or a special

clinic at a hospital would do one for you. But you'd best not get into that kind of trouble, anyways.'

Because I was interested, Miranda's mum gave me a leaflet from her hospital. It's got a good style – easy to read. I feel I could use this.

Acquired Immune Deficiency Syndrome, or AIDS

What is AIDS caused by?

AIDS is an infectious disease caused by a virus which gets into the cells of the body. A person who is infected will carry the virus for life. It is called HIV – Human Immunodeficiency Virus. This name is used because the virus infects and destroys cells of the immune system which normally protect the body against infections and cancers.

How is the virus spread?

It is spread in four ways:

1 Sexual intercourse The virus can be present in semen (sperm) and in the fluid in the vagina. Therefore it can be spread from a man to a woman, or from a woman to a man – during sexual intercourse. Men who are homosexuals and have anal intercourse with other men can spread the infection this way. AIDS is no different from any other 'sexually transmitted disease' (syphilis, gonorrhoea or herpes) so prostitutes and people who have many sexual partners run an especially high risk of being infected by the AIDS virus. You can also get it from oral sex, from either a man or a woman who is infected.

2 Injections The AIDS virus is spread by sharing injection equipment. Therefore people who inject drugs, such as heroin, and share needles, run a really serious risk.

3 Mothers to babies Babies can be infected by their mothers. If a woman is infected with the AIDS virus, there is a good chance that her baby will get the virus. The infection can be passed on to the baby in the womb.

4 Transfusions The virus can be transmitted in blood transfusions or in substances obtained from the blood (like those used for treating haemophiliacs). In this country this is now extremely rare, because all donated blood is tested for the virus, but this is not the case in all countries.

What happens when a person first gets infected with the virus?

The virus is in the body, but the person looks and feels well. It usually takes about three months after the virus gets into the body before the blood tests for the virus become positive. At this stage a person is known to be 'AIDS positive', 'an AIDS carrier', 'HIV positive' or 'body positive'. The person in this condition is infectious. He or she can spread the virus.

What happens next?

The virus starts to damage the body's immunity against infections and cancers. The person may feel tired, have enlarged glands (lumps in the neck, armpits or groin), sweat a lot, and get a lot of infections. None of these problems are unique to someone with AIDS. They can have many other causes. The person needs to see a doctor and have blood tests to sort out the reason. The person is still spreading the virus to other people.

The virus may also start to affect the brain and cause the person to behave strangely or get depressed. Later on, the person infected with the virus may develop cancers.

When does a person actually have AIDS disease?

A person is said to have 'AIDS disease' as distinct from being 'positive' or 'a carrier' when he or she shows signs of being ill from the AIDS virus.

Does everyone who gets the HIV infection get AIDS?

Probably 'yes', though it can take anything from a few months to many years from the time a person is first infected. A positive test for the HIV virus means that there is real risk of developing AIDS disease eventually, but the person may stay well for quite a few years. People infected with the AIDS virus can pass it on from the moment they get infected until they die.

How many people have AIDS and how many people have the virus but have not yet become ill?

The HIV iceberg: the world by end of 1989

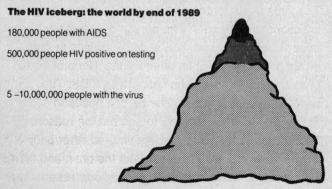

180,000 people with AIDS

500,000 people HIV positive on testing

5 –10,000,000 people with the virus

Is there a cure for AIDS?
At the present time, there is no cure.

Dad may have forgiven me – but the police are still chasing. At six this evening I was hauled in again. Dad came too. We walked into the station and this plod said, 'Right, we want you to know what's happening. You're here for further questioning about possession, growing, and dealing in drugs. Will you come with me, please?'

They took me away from Dad and put me in a police cell. They tried to get me to admit that Tony was the person who'd supplied me with the plant. (He was, but I wasn't going to tell them.) This time they were interviewing with a tape-recorder, and were being sort of bored asking about it and getting all the details like how high the plant was. By now I'd admitted I'd grown it – because I didn't want to get Tony into trouble. Can't think why, because he'd never do the same thing for me. When I refused to give any names, they said, 'Right, we'll leave you in the cell till you change your mind.'

I was in there for about an hour, and they were smoking away outside on fags. I nearly told them that if anything, *they* were the ones who were hooked. Then they brought me out and said, 'Right, have you changed your mind?' I said 'no' – so they put me back in again. Eventually I banged on the door and said I had to go to the toilet. This policewoman came and watched me, which wasn't very nice. Finally Dad complained and they let me go. Dad got a lecture too about his responsibilities. It was really great seeing Dad stick up for me like he did.

Afterwards I talked about it with my mates. We started blaming each other for giving names to the police which was ridiculous because none of us had. There was a lot of talk about whether we would go to court, and what the sentence would be or the fines. Dad was angry at being told off as well. He doesn't want me to see Tony any more because he thinks it's all Tony's fault that I got involved. But I'm going to ring him up. I want to know what hassle he's been getting, and I want to tell him the police didn't get any information out of me.

I have to admit that in respect of the police being so heavy, well maybe it was good what they did. I definitely won't smoke dope again – because if I'm caught, I'll be for it.

12 The hunk hangs it on Miranda

It's lucky I left school, or I'd have been down the cop shop like the rest of my old mates. They've nearly all been arrested for drugs or stealing bicycles (poor old Steve – what with Rachel going off with Tony and now this). Wouldn't have done me any good getting into that scene – me being black and all that. Doesn't make any difference with my friends, but it's not worth putting to the test with the law.

I think Rach is quite jealous of me doing my course at the CFE in catering and management. I know she thinks it's good to try and get 'A' levels, but I want to get on and do something useful, and earn money to help my family out – Dad being unemployed and all the burden falling on Mum. I want to have qualifications like Mum – not like Aunt Jane, who told me the only reason she stuck with her husband was because she'd never qualified. If she had, she'd have been able to earn her own money and would have divorced him years ago. There are a lot of great people at the CFE, and I like being among more mature people – they treat you as an adult. This makes the school crowd seem a bit childish now – though I'm fond of Rach and Jerry – particularly Rach.

Looking back, all that they used to teach me at school in personal relationship classes seems a bit mild. At the CFE, I do Course 409 on 'Life Skills' – taught by this really gorgeous upfront hunk, which is maybe why everyone goes to it. Anyhow, he knows the information backwards and gives it straight. At school the teacher would be coy, and would refer to a penis as 'the male member'. Last week at the CFE it was everyone's favourite subject these days – AIDS. It's amazing how a four-letter word can bring so much fear to the minds of people who hear it.

The hunk started by telling us some theories of where the virus came from that he had got from his last class. One was that it had come from an extra-terrestrial source (maybe the Martians have AIDS and sent a survivor to earth or it came down the phone line when ET phoned home). I told him that my friend's mum thinks it was a nuclear explosion that had started it all off. Another idea was that it had escaped from a germ warfare laboratory.

He then told us that the most likely scientific theory of where AIDS started was the 'green monkey' one. A virus exists in a species of monkey in Africa which, although it doesn't make the monkey ill, is a very similar virus to the AIDS one. What might have happened is that someone got bitten or scratched by one of these monkeys (or got up to something worse with them, I say), and the virus got across to their body, where it changed slightly into the one that causes AIDS. Although the virus was present in Africa for some time, making people ill, it wasn't until it got to America that people began to notice that there was a new disease around. It is thought it got to America in the blood of an airline steward who had slept with a man in Africa who had the virus. When he flew back to America, he spread it to all his homosexual friends, like a chain letter. (A more effective one than the chain letters I try and take part in.)

The hunk made it sound like a good 'who dunnit' detective story. But unlike the normal 'who dunnit' crimes you read about they may never find out where the AIDS virus actually came from. (More like the

70 per cent of crimes reported to the metropolitan police that stay unsolved.)

We spent the second half of the lesson inventing ways of giving condoms more street cred. The hunk said that the whole French army is being issued with dinky bright yellow condom holders, and they are being trained in pistol practice and condom practice at the same time. In the States they are putting them in fortune cookies and Christmas crackers, having little dispensers attached to key-rings, and making them into ear-rings. They even have specially designed holders for your filofax – as if it is no different from carrying around your felt-tip pen.

Afterwards we had a discussion with him as to whether he thought that if girls carried condoms around with them they'd be thought of as slags – cheap, forward and easy lays. Definitely not, he said, just good common sense – and why not make boys excited by carrying ten? I agree. People should accept that girls who carry a condom are not always looking for someone to jump into bed with, they're just being prepared for a special moment in their lives.

Poor Rach is really wary of men and their attitudes towards sex and women. Her experiences with Tony haven't helped much either. She's dead worried over how she can be sure that even one partner won't be HIV positive. She thinks that men might lie about their previous sexual exploits and say they've had less partners than they have – just to gain what they want.

I don't want AIDS to be another wet cloth in the face of my future relationships. To me sex is the most natural thing out, with the right person. And I don't think that the risk of AIDS should stop people from having sex. I agree with my friend Jo who says that it's OK as long as you take the right precautions, or as she puts it, 'A man wearing a rubber johnny is the best thing I know of.' She's got no time for people who say, 'Don't ever have sex so you don't catch AIDS,' and says, 'After all, if we didn't have a good bonk now and then, none of us would be here, would we?'

13 Me *and my mates*

Lying in bed this morning, I made a quick survey of
the damage of the last two days: (1) Amazing racing
bike repossessed – wonder if I'll ever have another
one like it? Total lack of sympathy from my parents
because of all the other hassles. (2) No money – but
Dad says I've got to have his jacket cleaned as it
stinks of smoke. Total injustice as I don't smoke. (3)
One pair of 501s with pocket torn from trying the
impossible with my rear bike light. (4) One heavily

damaged ego from Rachel going off with Tony like that. (5) Guilt to the eyeballs over the drink at the party and the damage that caused.

I decided that at least things couldn't get worse, that is until I had to face my sister Di across the breakfast table, and was appalled to find that she'd heard it *all* down to the very last juicy detail – and she couldn't believe that I wasn't involved. No way was I going to let her know that I'd been responsible for the buying of the vodka – though she has this nasty way of finding things out. Does she go in for third-degree torture I wonder? Mum seems to have conveniently forgotten our shopping expedition – a habit golden oldies have from time to time, though only when it's convenient for them. This time it was handy for both of us. I prayed she wouldn't make any remark to motor-mouth or the broadcasting system would be in action and a huge hand with a pointing finger would come down out of the sky – at me.

Later on I was round at Miranda's hearing more about the Sue and Paul saga (from Paul). I'd already heard it all from Rachel but tried to sound interested though my mind was really wrapped around my own problems. Other people's relationship problems are so incredibly boring. David was there as well, and was definitely interested. Maybe he's practising for sainthood – though none of us will believe it after his and Jerry's act together. Jerry swore after the party never to talk to Tony again, and Tony thinks

Jerry totally to blame for him being dragged down to the police station. I'm glad I managed to avoid all that.

There was a time when I quite fancied Jerry myself – but then this nagging fear came back of what I might catch. Bloody hell – I really don't want to have to think about all those diseases we've been taught about at school. I want to get on and enjoy sex (when it finally happens) and life (when that finally happens too) – not spend the whole time wondering what I'm going to catch. I mean, sex is a very confusing thing. In order for us to reproduce and survive as a human race, we have to have sex (though I'm not sure that I would give this as my number one reason!). Yet now I'm told that when I have sex I've not only got to worry about getting someone pregnant (which is needed for the human race to reproduce) but also

about herpes, gonorrhoea, chlamydia, non-specific urethritis, genital warts and God knows what else, as well as AIDS (which only helps nasty bugs reproduce). I mean, how do I balance these things off? And just what are the risks of getting one of those infections from, say, Rachel? (Not that I think she's the kind to have any of those things, which is one reason why I like her.)

Why have we had to inherit a polluted world from the previous generations? If it's not diseases transmitted by having sex, it's radiation due to the destruction of the ozone layer, or our oxygen disappearing because of the destruction of the rain forests, or pollution in rivers from greedy multinational corporations dumping chemicals. I thought that adults were meant to be responsible and mature.

David and I had one of our ongoing heavy discussions – is man a moral being? On the one hand he seems to have learnt to be a social creature and have some consideration for those around him, on the other he seems to be totally selfish and have no consideration about spoiling the environment he lives in. So the answer must be somewhere between the two. We all agreed that Tony was the prime example of having no regard for others, though I doubt whether he'd agree. Whatever he is, he's a liar – at least I hope he is, and not Rachel. This morning he was suggesting that Rachel went the whole way – he must have known how much he was hurting me –

whereas Rachel said she walked out on him at Adrian's party when he'd hardly even started.

I suggested to David and Paul that all this would never have happened (including me getting the vodka) if Mr Smythe hadn't been off ill. David and Paul just looked at one another and then both said, at the same time, 'Christ, haven't you heard . . . ?'

At this point the doorbell went, and in walked Tony and Jerry. This drugs business must have got them back together again. Jerry burst out, 'I was hauled into the station again today. They put me in this stinking cold police cell and tried to get me to admit that Tony here was the person who had supplied me with the plant. I didn't admit a thing. Eventually they let me go and said this wasn't the end of it.' Tony seemed totally unmoved by Jerry's story, ungrateful, and his usual shitty self. Why does she put up with him? Paul finally managed to finish the sentence he and David had begun before the interruption. 'Smythe died yesterday.'

I was stunned. Even Tony turned white and burst out, 'You're joking. That's not a nice thing to joke about. Don't do that to me.' Paul said, 'I'm not – honest. Look, it's in the local paper.' And it was. 'Stewart Smythe, the chemistry master at St. Oriel's School, died yesterday at Brasenose Hospital. A memorial service will be held at St Crispin's Church.' Dead. I'd seen him only two weeks before. It suddenly occurred to me that Brasenose Hospital had the unit

where Miranda's mum worked.

It must be totally horrendous having AIDS and knowing that you are going to die. I mean, I know we are all going to die in the long run, but we don't know when. Knowing one is going to die soon must be terrible.

Paul's reaction was that it served the dirty bugger right that he'd kicked the bucket. He thought that homosexuals who slept with other men and got AIDS were disgusting.

David went berserk. 'OK, so we know that the world we are growing up in today is pretty corrupt. AIDS has come to the forefront, and it *is* because of the way that men and women have chosen to live; but it doesn't mean that you have to blame the gays

– or anyone else for that matter. This doctor who spoke to our church group, his approach was, "If you don't want to put yourselves at risk, well, you've got the guidelines in the Bible." He said God didn't intend us to live the way we're living today.'

David was so worked up he couldn't stop. 'I wouldn't personally say this is a punishment from God – I don't feel that. But through what I've read in the Bible and what I've come to understand, I'm not surprised AIDS has happened because we've come so far from what He wants us to be like. My own response is that I want to get among the AIDS victims and help them, in no way cast them out but in no way also accept the way they were living their lives. I don't think AIDS is a punishment from God, because I don't think God likes to see suffering. It's sad they didn't take more care, but I wouldn't say "well, tough luck", though I might think it.

'One thing I have to agree with is that a Christian can't accept the homosexual way of life, but I don't condemn them because it's not my place to condemn. Right from the beginning, in Genesis, the Bible says that homosexuality is vile. It says that man and woman were created differently in order to have the capacity to love. I mean, maybe I might *feel* something for another boy, and might want to do something with him that I know the Bible says is wrong. But I have the choice, don't I? The thing with me is that I actually do have a guide to tell me what is right and wrong, and if I did go ahead then I'd know it was wrong. I don't agree with Charlie's so-called "Christian" view that it's OK to sleep around as long as you wear a condom. But someone who wasn't a Christian and didn't believe might not know that they were doing wrong in quite the same way.'

Some of this seemed pretty confused to me. I don't know whether there's a God or not, and even if there is, I don't know that any of this would be to do with him. It seems to me that everyone has to make their own decision about what they want to do or not do. The main thing is not to allow people to force you to do things you don't want to do. It is also important not to hurt other people, or put anyone else at risk.

Maybe when I leave school I will also want to work with prostitutes and drug users, and other people who are having a bad time. I mean — it's not always their fault.

By this time, the gathering was becoming like a disorganized school reunion. Rach arrived, looking like a 'born again' version of herself. She totally ignored Tony — he might just as well not have been there. She was very friendly to me however. I'm deeply suspicious that I'm just being used by her as a 'Star Wars offensive system'. Not that Tony noticed. He was much too wrapped up with his own ego and Jerry's body.

The subject of AIDS drifted on. Rach had also heard about Mr Smythe. When it happens to someone close to you it brings it home hard. We just couldn't stay away from it. We started on other things, but always came back. Tony was disgusting – no respect and full of awful jokes. 'What does AIDS stand for?' 'Anally injected death syndrome.' 'Have you heard the one about the Irishman? There was a Scotsman, an Englishman and an Irishman, all of whom were intravenous drug users. The Scotsman and the Englishman used clean needles each time they injected themselves. The Irishman didn't bother, just used any old dirty needle. The Scotsman and the Englishman were horrified and asked him why he took such risks. "Ah," he said, "don't you worry your heads. I'm fully protected against catching AIDS. I'm wearing a condom." ' Maybe making jokes is Tony's way of dealing with fear of AIDS.

When we were first told about AIDS and it was brought out into the open, people were really worried. But they haven't changed the way they carry on and still go around having sex with just about everyone. I think that those government adverts on TV were really good and scary. I bet they made people think a bit more before sleeping around or sharing needles. But it seems to me that one minute everything you watch is all about AIDS, and then it stops being newsworthy and drifts to the back of people's minds. Though everyone is always saying to me, 'Remember to use a condom', as if I have to wear a condom whatever I'm doing – driving a car, doing the washing-up, eating at McDonalds. I suppose I should pop one on even when I'm just taking a girl out to eat at McDonalds? 'Well, dear, you never know what might happen. Perhaps you'll get carried away over a Big Mac.'

14 Back from the future

Steve

Got his 'A' levels and went to Liverpool Polytechnic to study hydrology. While there, he got involved with an AIDS support group. He had two relationships with other students, one of which was sexual. However he never lost his longing and affection for Rachel and continued to write to her. When he left the poly he joined the Voluntary Service Overseas and is now teaching the basics of irrigation on a project near Kaoma in Zambia. He still writes to Rachel about life in Africa though he is now married to a local woman (a fact he doesn't mention in his correspondence). Living as he does, in a country where in some clinics up to 50 per cent of women attending for pregnancy care are found to be HIV positive, he realizes that the original fears about the spread of AIDS were well founded. In Africa, from the start, the disease seems to have affected men and women equally.

Rachel

Took her 'A' levels and went to Bristol University to study law. While there, she fell in love with another law student and got married. Their first child was born while she was 'in Chambers'. She called the child 'Steve' much to the bewilderment of her husband who wanted the name 'Anthony'. She rarely answers the letters that come to her from Africa, knowing as she does – from a mutual friend – that Steve is married. Having become known among her colleagues as a feminist fighting to get a decent deal for women lawyers, she now specializes in getting financial settlements from the government for haemophiliacs with AIDS.

Tony

Dropped out of school completely a few weeks after the party. The reconciliation with Jerry was only temporary and their relationship ended. He started work in the local branch of the Pizza Hut but was fired after two weeks because of 'persistent aggression to those in authority'. After a series of further jobs, each lasting less than three days, he became permanently unemployed. He's now a heroin addict, a habit he supports by supplying to other addicts. He's already had one test for HIV which was negative and is now awaiting the results of his second test. His mother has remarried a man who runs a local chemist's shop. He and Tony do not get on and Tony is living in a squat in London. He occasionally visits home. When he does his friends still gather, but his charm is wearing thin and after one outing together there is general relief when he returns to London. During these occasional trips home, he visits Mr Smythe's grave in the local graveyard. He never tells anyone about this.

David

After leaving school, started to study theology at a seminary on the outskirts of Leeds. However, after two months, much to his parents' disappointment, he became an agnostic humanist. At the same time, he became involved with a 'Jerry-like' woman whom he had met while doing good works with a local church group. She already had a daughter aged four by a previous liaison. She then became pregnant by David and when she was five months pregnant they got married. David now works as a garage mechanic and is still involved with the local group which is beginning to see more AIDS cases among its clientele.

Jerry

Was let off by the police with a caution. Two months later her father suffered a severe heart attack and was in and out of hospital for a month. Jerry therefore decided to delay her trip around the world and to finish her typing course instead. She helped look after her father while he was at home, but he subsequently died. His will specified that Jerry should use £1,500 of her inheritance to travel. She married an Australian businessman and started delivering single-seater aircraft to remote parts of the outback. None of her friends has heard from her for years, and, although they don't know it, she was killed when she crashed three hundred miles north of Alice Springs. Her body was never found.

Miranda

Finished at the CFE and began work in a local bank. Her mother became ill and had to retire from work. At first Rachel and Jerry were afraid that she had caught AIDS. Miranda was worried about her being ill, but not about it being AIDS. She knew from her mother that of the 182,463 cases in the world at the moment, only a handful had caught the virus from working with people with AIDS. As it turned out, she had breast cancer, which was successfully treated. Miranda slowly worked her way up the banking ladder and is now manager of a major branch. She has had various relationships but values her independence and continues to live alone.